IN-LINE SKATING

Written by Mike Saiz

TOP THAT!

Copyright © 2002 Top That! Publishing plc
Tide Mill Way, Woodbridge, Suffolk, IP12 1AP, UK www.topthatpublishing.com
Top That! is a Registered Trademark of Top That! Publishing plc

24 Contents

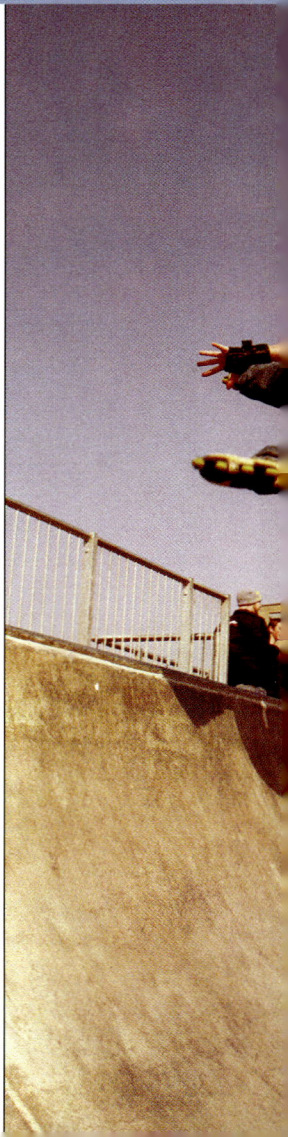

**It seems that wherever you go –
be it for a stroll in the park, a
walk along a beach promenade
or through a town centre –
you'll see in-line skaters.**

Four Types

The sport is clearly
divided into four types:
recreational, aggressive,
roller hockey and
speed skating. Whether
you're in it just for
fun or you want to
compete, in-line skating
is an enjoyable and
skilful way to keep fit.

The Big Questions

So what do you need
to become an in-line
skater? What skills
must be learnt, and
how much will it cost?
Over the course of
this book, all these
questions and many
others will be
answered and you will
soon be skating with
style and in safety.

Make the Effort

A little determination
and perspiration will
take you from being a
bunny to a stair-
bashing, hardcore
skater. Use the
glossary at the back of
this book if you want
to check the meanings
of any of the skater-
speak words used.

If some skerds (skate nerds) start claiming stuff, bust a few of these facts to stop them in their tracks.

Origins

It is generally believed that people in northern Europe, unable to ice skate in the warmer months, slapped wheels onto their winter skates to carry on carving. That was 300 years ago!

The First Skate

The first skate to resemble an in-line was invented by John Joseph Merlin, a Belgian born in 1735. By today's standards the design looked quite crude, with metal wheels.

Merlin

Merlin was one hardcore guy, and allegedly busted a party wide open by crashing in and slamming fine-style into a huge mirror, unable to steer or stop. Technology has moved on a bit since then.

The First Patent

The first patent for a roller skate was taken out by M Petitbled in Paris, France in 1819. The 'Petitbled' featured three in-line wheels on a wooden plate and leather straps to fasten them onto the foot. The wheels were available in three types, to allow a range of feel and traction:

Wood – nice mellow ride, plenty of grip, excellent fitness wheel;

Ivory – good all-round wheel, best for riding chuddy sidewalk and gentle bowls;

Metal – good for hardcore vert and street. These babies could take a savage session and still come back for more.

The Five-Wheel Boot

In 1823 in England, a boot with five wheels was developed by Robert Tyres. But it wasn't until the 1860s that a decent boot with wheels attached to the chassis was created. This stopped them from wobbling so much. After this development many of the skates were arranged in the 2 + 2 style, or 'quad' as it is called today.

Ball-Bearing Wheels

The biggest breakthrough came in 1884, with the invention of ball-bearing wheels. This provided a smoother ride and gave people the confidence to try

tricks including skating backwards. But don't forget – all this was still over 100 years ago! Over the years, small advances to quad skates made them more comfortable and easier to ride.

The In-line Skate

By 1960 the Chicago Skate Company was marketing an in-line boot that looks much like the ones available today. Alas, the boot was not comfortable and had no brake, so was all but forgotten.

The in-line skate as we know it was not created until 1979, when Scott Olson, an ice hockey player from

Minneapolis, USA, bought a pair of skates and took them home to work on them. He recognised exactly what those crazy guys in northern Europe had all those years ago and saw that these beauties could be used off-season to practise hot manoeuvres ready for the new season.

Invention

He modified this skate, adding better wheels and a brake. He soon realised he was onto something and began marketing his 'invention', realising there was plenty of tarmac to bang on.

5

The Explosion

The big in-line explosion happened in the 1980s. In America, masses of people were taking up the sport, opting mostly for hockey and recreational skating. It's a great way of getting from A to B and exercising in an urban environment as, let's face it, there's a lot of pavement to be had, not to mention the beach front and parks.

Rollerblade

Olson's company was bought by Bob Neagele Jr, who formed Rollerblade Inc. in 1984 (hence a lot of in-line skates are called 'blades'). People wanted the new boots for training and keep-fit aerobic low-impact exercise, but more importantly a new type of sport was born: aggressive skating. This was closely related to skateboarding whose enthusiasts really helped push the technology and sport to the limit.

Terminology

First, and this is very important, don't say "I'm just popping out to do a spot of rollerblading." Rollerblades are in-line skates, but not all skates are rollerblades, OK? As was once said, "Rollerblading ain't a word, although some people continue to use it. The people who work at Rollerblade call it 'SKATING'." Don't get confused about this point, or you will live your life blading and probably end up a gherkin.

Trivia

In the early days, and we are talking early here, there were specific skates for men and women. Women's had heels — yes, you have read that right, heels — but all skates had metal wheels, dodgy bindings and no brake.

But now when you slap on a pair of boots, you know that the materials have been tested on the streets to destruction, that they are safe and will stand plenty of gnarly action.

Fitness

Skating is a good way of getting fit. It's a low-impact sport so that means no mashed-up knees, hips and ankles, and it burns tons of calories (500–900 an hour depending on how hard you skate). A good tip for all you stair-bashers and hardcore skaters alike — when you pack your backpack for a day's sessioning, pack food and plenty of water because you will need lots of refreshment to keep you going.

became the most popular form as more and more skaters sessioned on the concrete, tarmac, handrails, kerbs and stairs. In fact it's so popular now, most towns have specialised areas set aside for the sport which become very busy at the weekends and holidays.

Aggressive

For a while in the 1980s, there were millions of people out in their spandex, shades and bum bags looking cool and everyone was happy – especially the skate manufacturers. Then a shift occurred. A subculture of aggressive skaters started pushing the sport into a different area. These skaters embraced the urban environment to the max and changed the sport, bringing their own language and style. Aggressive

Popularity

Skating is now seriously big business, and the main stars of the sport can earn millions from sponsorship and competitions. It keeps sucking new groms in with the fever, but this is good as they are the stars of tomorrow. It is estimated that there are over 30 million in-line skaters around the world today. In 1997, nearly

4 million pairs of quality skates were sold in Europe alone. It's not just kids' stuff, either – the average age of a skater is 25.

Safety

You've got to be careful, too. Most commonly, skaters sustain injury to their wrists and hands – 37% of all injuries sustained from the sport are to these areas. The least common but potentially most dangerous injuries occur to the head, where 5% of injuries happen. If you are unlucky enough to face-plant, you are in the 8%. Always wear protective clothing and pads when you skate – you know it makes sense.

Crash and Burn

Don't worry if you crash and burn a lot while you learn — as long as your armour is in place, you shouldn't get too much road rash. Also, if you have your kit sorted you will feel more confident about trying new stunts and tricks, and so become a skater so good people will be awed! Got that nailed? Then read on…

Choice used to be limited, not by the skates, but by the other equipment necessary. Only when people began to couple new materials with the in-line boot did the full potential of skating become apparent.

Aggressive Skating

There are two types of aggressive skating: street and vert. Street skaters are urban gymnasts, who grind, jump and ride almost anything, from stair rails and kerbs to park benches and pillar boxes. This group of skaters are the most visible to the perps and are the ones that get the gherkins waving their fists.

Vert

Vert riders use specially constructed ramps, quarterpipes and specialised sections and boxes. There is some crossover between the groups but a seasoned vert rider will give it up when he pulls massive air and lands it butter-style.

Recreational Skating

This was the most popular form until aggressive took over that title. It's a low-impact, calorie-burning, fun sport. You can go anywhere – on smooth tarmac or pavements.

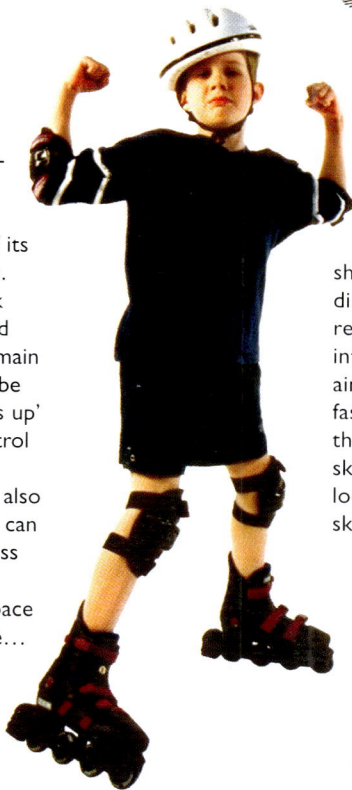

In-line Hockey

This sport is BIG. Sometimes called street hockey, it is played by very fast-footed, fit teams with all the competitiveness of its counterpart on ice. Skill and teamwork make this a fast and furious game. The main skill required is to be able to skate 'heads up' whilst keeping control of the puck or ball with your stick. It's also pretty handy if you can turn on a penny, pass and shoot and still keep up a furious pace for the entire game… not for the faint-hearted!

Speed Skating

Funnily enough, the object is speed! You race short or long distances, either in regular races, timed intervals or solo. The aim is to clock the fastest time or win the race. Speed skaters dress with the look of speed ice skaters or cyclists.

A little extra help with armour is a good idea. You will see loads of skaters tearing up the ramps, fun boxes and streets without much in the way of safety gear on at all. Well, these hardcore types are taking calculated risks about the tricks they perform. You shouldn't try to follow suit.

Kitting Out

Give yourself a confident start (and a relatively painless one) by slapping on some pads and a lid (helmet). You will find your learning curve greatly improved when there is no fear of smashing your body every time you take a spill.

Wrist Guards

The plastic splints that support the wrists help to break your fall. These are absolute essentials; buy them and then you shouldn't have to spend months in plaster.

Elbow Pads

The Velcro pads fasten above and below the elbow with a hardened outer shell, giving extra protection on impact.

Knee Pads

As with many elbow pads, some knee pads have extra protection on the sides to protect your joints. These are essential when vert riding for a safe escape from failed tricks, and are also vital for hockey.

Helmet

It's essential to protect your head, as an injury here could do you long-term damage. Make sure it fits well and comes down far enough to protect the back of your head.

Clothing

Choose garb that will best perform and protect your body for the type of skating you choose. Loose, hard-wearing and baggy-as-you-like cool stuff is best for aggressive skating; light, stretchy and cool for speed skating and as much protection as you can get for hockey.

Health Warning

You should NEVER skate… in traffic, on private property, in the dark, on gravel, in the wet, alone, when people don't know where you are or where you're going. All these will get you into the face-plant, scrape-school of road rash hell faster than you can say jack.

One last bit of advice: spend as much as you can on your skates, as these babies are what will keep you stoked and enjoying the sport.

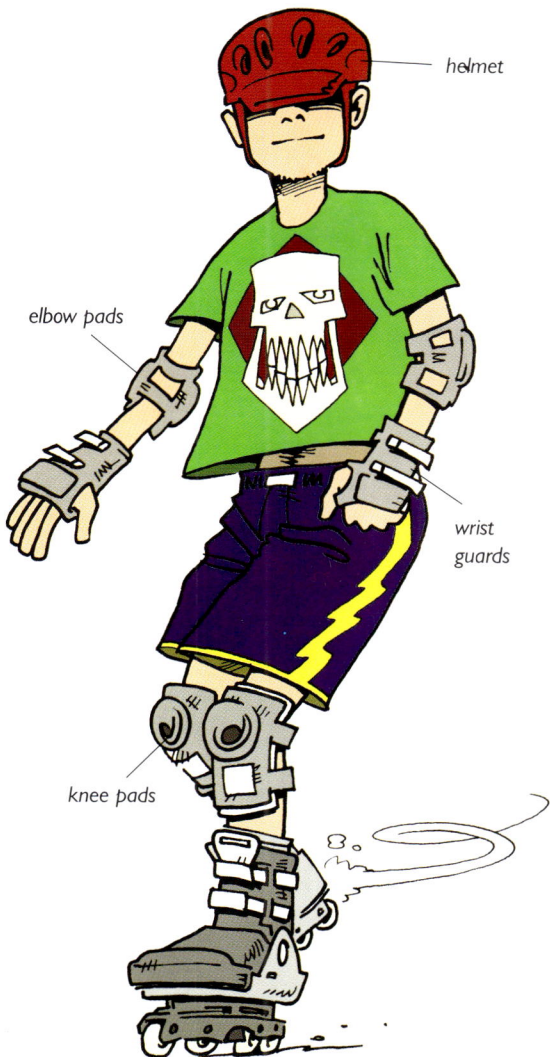

helmet

elbow pads

wrist guards

knee pads

Let's be honest, now – you will hit the deck at some point, get bashed up and bleed a bit, but then if it was that easy, we would be born with wheels and not feet, right? A little bit of light warming up and a few tricks of the trade will ensure you minimise the damage, though.

Warm Up
You do not have to do this in front of anybody; do it before you go out, either in your house, your garage or in a dark cupboard. Lightly stretch your legs, back and sides to make sure your muscles are ready to deal with the onslaught of exercise. Gearing up properly for a session could make all the difference between landing that phat brainless or being laid up with an ice pack on your knee after a gnarly kerb hop. So be warned.

Water
If you take a backpack with you, take some water, not just to drink but in case you get a touch of road rash. A quick splash of water will clean it till more effective measures can be taken to dress the wound. If you hurt your head at any time, check yourself, and seek medical help if you are cut, black out

or are seeing stars. In short and for want of a better expression, use your head.

How To Fall

One last tip – keep your body weight forward when you learn, with your legs slightly bent. If you fall in this position, it will be forwards, avoiding the shame of a bizarre windmilling-arm action and cartoon-legged backside wipeout… not cool.

Whether you're a total grom or a seasoned pro, the skates you choose will influence how much you enjoy the sport.

Skate Types

All in-line skates are made up of the same basic elements, but each is tailored to a different type of skating. Start with recreational, because these are vanilla. If you want to specialise after that your hard-earned dosh will not have been wasted, because the skills you will have learnt on these will be just as applicable on a specialist skate.

Recreational Skates

If you want skates as a means of just getting around, the rec is for you. At first glance, you see the brake at the back and big wheels (measuring around 70–80 mm). This is cool because big wheels mean speed. Check out the illustration below to examine the breakdown further. It's fair to say that if you buy the most expensive pair you can afford, you'll be doing yourself a favour.

Cheap Skates

Buying cheap skates is false economy and even though you may have to pinch yourself when you see the price tag, a good pair will serve you well and give you a certain amount of cred before you even start. Make sure they are comfortable from the word go, too.

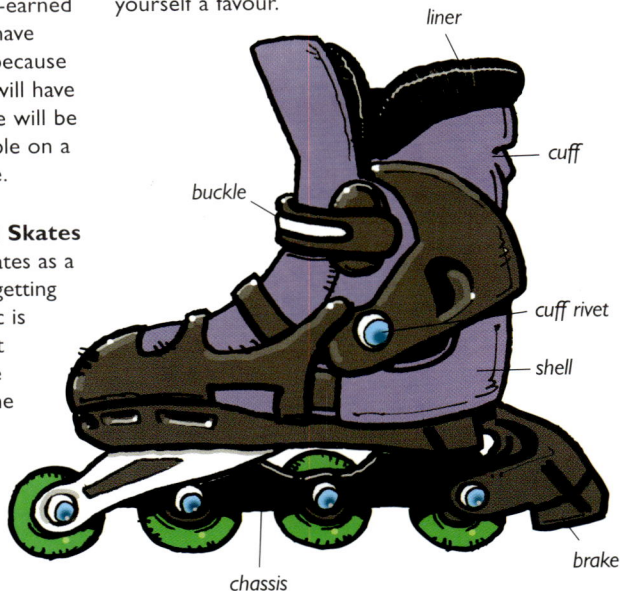

liner

cuff

buckle

cuff rivet

shell

brake

chassis

Aggressive Skates

Just as its name suggests, aggressive is a pumping, physical and potentially dangerous type of skating. If this is not for you, stop reading here and skip to the last two types of skate.

Look at these suckers. From the outset, you can see these have been built to take punishment. They are robust, have grind plates and smaller, harder wheels, usually measuring around 48–55 mm. Yep – these mints are your one-way ticket to hardcore skating. Check the spec below so you know what to look for when choosing a pair of these bad boys:

- small, hard wheels
- a chassis with replaceable parts
- a hard shell
- fasteners (lace or buckle) that don't protrude
- removable liner
- no brake

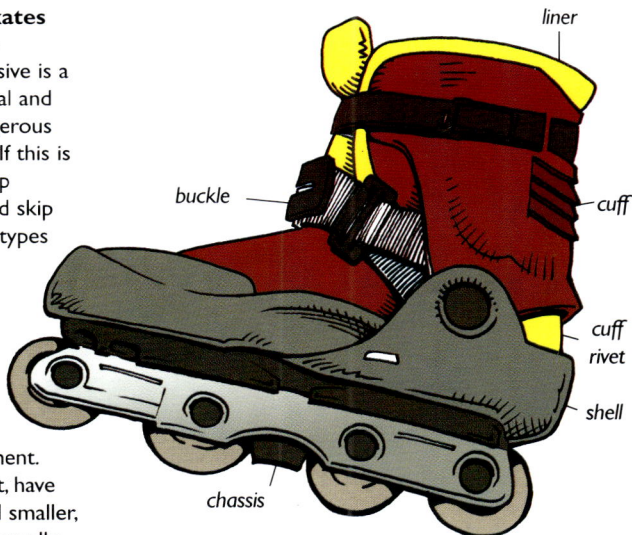

liner

buckle

cuff

cuff rivet

shell

chassis

Speed Skates

The first thing you notice about these skates is that they have five very hard, big wheels, each measuring around 80 mm. Unlike the other skates we have looked at, the boot section on a speed skate is lightweight to make it more aerodynamic and has a more trainer-like look.

Speed skating is not for the faint-hearted. You'll need to be superfit and have a healthy bank balance to afford to compete; this sport is very similar to ice skating, and is quite expensive to enjoy.

Hockey Skates

These skates are the direct descendants of ice skates and are where in-lining began. The thing you'll notice about these skates is that there are no clips or straps, just laces, and that they still look like a boot on an ice skate. Just like their specialised cousin, the speed skate, hockey skates will put a serious dent in your bank balance, but they're built to last.

liner

cuff

laces

shell

chassis

As is the case with more formal hockey, 'pick-up hockey' or 'street hockey' is great fun but requires a lot of skill as you have to cope with not only skating, but also manoeuvring a hockey stick. In trying to score goals, you must avoid other skaters. One last thing to consider, if you get bitten by the hockey bug, is that to join an affiliated league you may have to buy a serious amount of kit.

By the time you go to buy your first skates, you may have already hired or borrowed some boots and got the fever. You know what you want, but what about the specifics? What are the pros and cons, how do you know you won't be ripped off?

Where to Start
If you don't have a good idea of what type of skating you want to do, a recreational pair is your best bet. One pair of recreational skates is much like another, so until you can be more specific about your requirements, stick with these.

Where to Buy
Do not buy from department stores, as they generally carry a limited range and the sales staff are unlikely to have the necessary knowledge about the skates or styles. By all means use these shops to compare prices but don't limit your search to here.

Buy from specialist skate shops where the owners will have a greater knowledge and a wider selection of skates and will be able to help you make the right decision. Buy armour the same time you buy your skates and make your purchase before the weather gets warm as the prices heat up also.

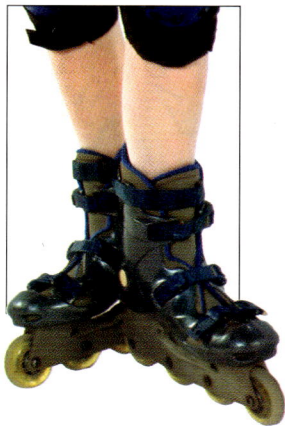

Buying Your First Skates

Buying Tips

Be prepared to invest in some decent skates though. Cheap skates are made from low-quality materials. Result? Foot pain, no ankle support, sluggish bearings and a rough ride. They are more likely to break, too. You don't want a detached wheel or broken buckle when you're pulling airtime.

What to Look For

The boots must fit well and be comfortable, as they won't 'give' much. They are meant to protect and support the foot and ankle. Leave both boots on in the shop for a while to get the feel of them. Stand about and even skate a bit if there is room.

Ratings

Check the ABC ratings on the bearings: generally speaking, the higher the number, the better (look for ABC5 or ABC7).

Make sure the wheels are the correct size and hardness for the type of skating you are going to do.

If You Still Can't Decide...

Ask the opinion of other skaters. They will not pull any punches on what they think of various brands and styles. Always remember: these boots are made to take a beating and perform at a high level. If they fail to do this, you are within your rights to demand a refund or exchange.

The very best place to start skating is flat, wide, smooth and quiet with a soft place to run off (slow down or stop) or crash. A park or beach promenade is perfect, but try not to go when it's packed solid.

Stance

Look at the illustration, right. Notice there are no straight limbs here; the skater's weight is thrown forward (no tipping back please). Do not look at your feet as you could face-plant, so look ahead – that's where the action is, after all! Relax and be loose. When you move away keep those limbs soft and relaxed. With your feet pointed in a 'V', gently push and shift your body weight forward.

Wipeout

This is an inevitable part of skating. If you feel you are going to fall, bend your knees. The aim is to get your body weight as near as possible to the ground before you do. Fall to your knees first, then shift your weight onto your wrist guards, before ending on your elbow pads. Shaken but not scathed, get up, dust off and start again!

Stroke and Glide

This is the key to moving and getting up speed.

Step 1

Get set in the starting stance. Move off by weight shifting and pushing your skate out then bringing it back to the start position. Repeat the move with your left foot.

Step 2

When your weight is on your right skate, hold it there and glide, before pushing off or stroking with the left foot. Repeat on the left foot. You have now completed a stroke and glide cycle.

Step 3

Once all this seems natural, roll along with your feet parallel, keeping your weight forward and your arms out in front. This is known as parallel rolling. Repeat steps 1 and 2 to gain speed, slowing gradually or taking a breather when you need to. See how long you can stay on one foot while rolling, but remember: do it on both legs and be confident on both feet.

Unless you enjoy barrelling into bushes, you need to learn how to stop. Being totally in control of stopping will boost your confidence enormously. You will be able to attack more serious terrain with confidence, and avoid injuring yourself.

Running Out

'Running out' involves stopping on a soft verge such as grass. This will stop you quickly and is a lot softer than tarmac. Keep your body loose and low when heading for the green. In an emergency, you can grab lampposts, railings or walls. In these instances protective gear is a must. Stopping this way is not advisable, but if you are ever forced to choose between a tree or an oncoming car, the tree should win every time!

Using the Brake

Using your brake is important, but don't expect it to stop you instantly. The brake will provide a gradual deceleration. If you are parallel rolling and you feel the need to slow down, start by making sure your arms are in front of you. Bring your brake foot forward, so the brake is about parallel with the toe on the other foot. Point your toes up on your brake foot, keeping your body low. Shift your weight forward to the heel of your brake foot, lean on it and you will slow down.

T-Stop

Basically you form a 'T' with your skates, as this picture shows. This is quite a radical stop and is not kind to your wheels, but when done properly will stop you quickly. Once you are in the 'T' shape, shift your weight onto your back leg and steer with your front foot. The dragging, trailing wheels act as your brake.

Snow Plough

Turn your skates into an inverted 'V' when you need to slow down. You may have to do a succession of ploughs to slow completely though, so this is not appropriate for emergency stopping.

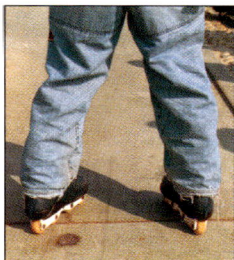

Hockey Stop and Power Slide

These two radical techniques are for stopping quickly. They require making fast turns and weight shifting. The hockey stop involves a sharp turn to the left and then the right, pushing your skates away from the centre of the turn. This makes your skate slide across the ground. The power slide involves spinning backwards whilst extending the other leg straight out and forcing it to slide along the ground.

Slalom

The slalom involves forming smooth, cool carves, gliding and shifting the weight. The pushing out on the corners is what slows you down.

Notice the position of the legs and how bent the left leg is. The watchword for these manoeuvres is commitment.

Your skates have been scientifically designed to carve, and knowing this and having confidence in the grip they give you will help you perform many radical turns.

The A-Frame

The A-frame turn is illustrated below. This is a weight shifting exercise. Stand as the illustration shows – weight evenly balanced. To go right, bend the left knee and push out. Once you have turned, stop by straightening the leg. To go left, follow the same procedure as above with the other leg.

The Crossover

The crossover turn, illustrated below, is a way of taking corners without slowing down. Coast into a turn, with most of your weight on your right foot if turning right (your left foot if turning left) as you lean in. For turning right, lift the left skate and cross it over the right one (the stepover), keeping your right leg bent. When the left skate is on the ground move the right skate into the normal position. This crossover can be repeated on a turn and you can pump out the skate to keep your speed up. Again, reverse the feet if turning left.

Learning to spin will help you to stop, but it's also a great way to enter and exit a trick.

Rotation and Spin Stops

Controlled rotation is essential as it lays the foundations for later tricks. It may sound obvious but look in the direction you are rotating.

Basic 360°
Step 1

First, decide which way you are going to spin. For spinning to the right, put your left skate heel up in the trailing position, with your right foot rolling nicely.

Step 2

Begin to turn your left knee outwards by using your foot as a pivot. This will force your legs apart and your right foot to turn and become the trailing foot.

Step 3

Put the left skate down (you should now be standing as in the illustration) and turn in a tightish circle.

Depending on the speed you go into a spin and how you apply the pressure to your skates, you can stop quickly or rotate to your heart's content. For stopping, think power slide, spread your legs wider and lean into the spin.

Do not worry if you spin out or stack it, just continue to practise. At first your feet may come out of alignment, or the force of spinning (at first quite weird) may cause you to lose your bearings and balance. So be cautious at first and then gradually add some mustard.

Pro Tip

Just a little note: if you've got this far and it's been easy, you may decide to ditch your brake. If your skating is getting more trick-laden and you can stop easily in a variety of ways, then you probably don't need it.

Skating backwards is another 'must do' move, as on the vert and street you must be able to go in or come out of a trick fakie, and it's essential when playing hockey. Not only that, it looks cool.

Step 4

Repeat the previous steps for continued motion.

Rocking

This is the move that will give you the feel and start you off rolling backwards. It's a very gentle in-and-out movement and will build your confidence.

Step 1

Start on a flat surface with your feet parallel and gently force your toes in (see illustration, right) and you will start to move backwards. Throughout this movement keep your knees bent.

Step 2

Push with the balls of your feet until you reach the point when you realise that you are about to lose control.

Step 3

Now is the time to turn your skates in and close that gap. This movement is like coasting and is a feely type of move that uses the balls of your feet and the inside edges of your skates.

Cabbing

This is a slightly more advanced way of skating backwards. It also allows you to twist your body more in the direction you are travelling so making it easier to see where you going.

Step 1

Start off again as with the rocking stance, but now lower yourself down a bit further and, as you do so, push your skates out using the inside edges.

Step 2

Bring your feet back in to the position shown in the illustration below and keep your skates on the ground.

Step 3

Now whichever foot you feel most comfortable with becomes the anchor foot. If it's your left foot, push out quite hard with your right foot (think kung fu kick here) and keep your toes pointing slightly inwards.

Step 4

After you've kicked out, start to pull your foot into the starting position but, using the front wheels of the anchor foot, repeat the motion with the right foot becoming the anchor. What's cool about this style of skating is that it gives you real power and you'll be able to skate up hills and round corners with control.

SEVEN

Fakie

The last type of backward skating is great to use just before setting up a trick and allows a great view as you are quite twisted.

Step 1

Once again you start off pushing away in a 'V'.

Step 2

Once you are moving, all your motion will be generated by one foot whilst the other acts as an anchor. Push off with your right foot (the left is your anchor) as shown in the illustration.

Step 3

As it reaches the outside, turn your skate and let it drift back.

Step 4

Once it has reached the front of the anchor foot, it's time to push out again. Think of the whole motion as carving question marks into the tarmac and keep it smooth. Once again this can be a gentle or speed-gathering way of going backwards.

When you can go backwards in a variety of ways, you are only a hop away from skating regular to fakie without stopping or slowing down and landing late 360°s on the vert.

Pro Tip

Before attempting phat moves off stair rails, practise on kerbs. Once mastered, you will soon be 360° rewinding off gnarly rails.

This section will take you a little closer to being a complete skater. You will learn to move on uneven surfaces and deal with kerbs, hills, jumping and stalls. This last move is the basis for a lot of vert and street moves.

Going Uphill
Don't lean back, keep your weight on the balls of your feet, keep your knees bent and use your arms for balance.

Going Downhill
Stay in control of your speed, don't let the hill dictate your descent by using big turns, traversing (think skiers on a hill) and weaving.

Obstacles
A lot of the time you can just skate round obstacles, but every once in a while, more drastic action is needed. You may have to jump over a pothole or log, and this can be accomplished by following the steps below.

Step 1
Glide towards the object, letting one foot lead slightly. As you get close to the object, bend your knees more, lean forward and put your arms back.

Step 2
At the point of take-off extend your legs and body and lift your arms, as though you are jumping on the spot.

Step 3
Just before landing, bend your knees to take the impact, and land with one skate slightly in front of the other for extra stability. Practise over various objects and heights to master this technique.

Kerbs

Don't practise this on a busy road and start slowly.

To mount a kerb, glide towards it, and as you get closer move one skate forward. Keep most of your weight on the back foot and raise the front foot a step up, shifting your weight onto the leading foot.

To come off a kerb, glide towards it and, as you get closer, move one skate forward. Keeping most of your weight centred, glide off the kerb with your knees bent to absorb the impact, and your arms out for balance.

Stalls

Stalls are the bread and butter of a lot of aggressive moves. When aggressive skaters are fully competent with jumping and stepping, stalls are a natural progression. Here is a stall walk-through. Pick a stair, for instance, skate slowly up to it and get ready to jump. Bear in mind you want to land both skates simultaneously between the second and third wheel, and hold it for a second or two. Jump off and skate away. Practise variations: go in fakie or try a 180° stall and 360° rewind.

① ②

Now you can stall, it's time to hit objects at more acute angles and greater speeds.

First Timer

Before grinding for the first time, make sure you have plenty of armour on and that your skates have grind plates. Start on something low, like a kerb. Remember it's the precision landing that makes the move; if you don't nail, you will bail. There are four basic types of grinds: frontside, backside, royale and soul.

Frontside Grind

Think kung fu kick type of stance and you're halfway there. Keep your weight centred and slide on your centre wheels along the rail (see picture, below). Land this beauty with your legs apart, and your back facing the rail. To exit, jump off in the direction you want to land.

Backside Grind

A variation on the frontside, but this time you face the rail. Approach as usual but as you jump, turn 180°, land facing the rail and slide between your centre wheels. Exiting the trick is more difficult as you can't see where you're going.

Royale Grind

Similar to the frontside, but this time most of your weight is on the back foot. Keep your back leg bent and face the direction you are going on the rail. Land this trick like the others and keep your centre of gravity low. To exit, the choice is yours, but do it smoothly.

Soul Grind

Royale Grind

Soul Grind

So called because you grind the soles of your skates. Approach the rail low and as you land, your back foot should tuck under you so the wheels are facing forward. Keep your weight on this back skate. To exit, twist your hips and straighten up at the same time.

Extra Moves

Once you've nailed these tricks and feel confident, add a true spin (forward spin on the approach), or a fakie spin (backward spin on the approach). You could even alley oop it (with your feet switched so your back foot now leads).

Watch other skaters and copy their moves as well, but don't overdo it as this isn't cool, and don't worry if you pull a few shockers yourself. Just make sure you land them all.

This is the place where you can pull it all together and really show your stuff. First, let's look at a basic ramp.

Ramp Terms

Flat – centre of ramp.

Transition – the bit that takes you from the flat to the vert.

Vert – this is where the action happens.

Coping – metal rails at the top for grinds, stalls and plants.

Deck – for dropping, bailing or chillin'.

Get the Feel

You will first have to get the feel of this beast, as it will be like nothing you have skated on before. So be sure to put all your armour on. It's best to start on a mini (like a vert but smaller), so when you fall, it won't be so far.

First, skate up to the transition keeping your legs bent and one foot slightly in front. Feel the speed drop off as gravity pulls you back and remain calm and relaxed. Next thing you know you have hit the other transition. Stay cool, ride it out and come back down.

After a while, get more speed up and try some mellow turns on the transition. Try skating in a figure 8, or fakie, but focus on getting confident and keeping it all smooth and relaxed.

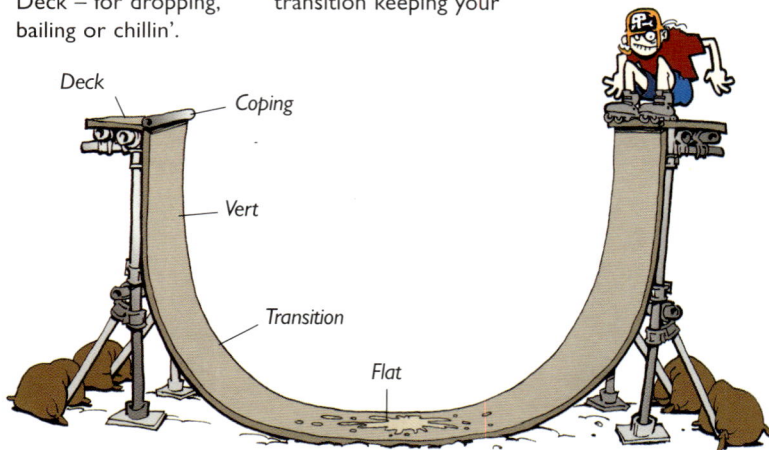

Deck
Coping
Vert
Transition
Flat

Dropping In

This basic 'trick' is a good place to start before you grind and throw in some 180°s, 360°s, handplants and more. Sit-ins and stand-ins are ways to drop in.

Sit-in

Before doing a full-on acid drop, try a sit-in as it will give you the confidence to try other drop-ins. Sit on the deck, place your hands either side of you and lift your backside up. Then let yourself fall off the deck, making sure all your wheels hit the vert at the same time.

It's a funny feeling, but doing it this way means if you slam it will be from a lesser height.

Stand-ins

Put one of your skates on the rail, the other on the deck. When you drop over, the rail foot becomes the trailing foot. When you go over do not push yourself out, just roll over. If you can do a sit-in you will know the feeling. Whatever you do don't lean back. Now that you know the moves, it's up to you to experiment. Get to know the feeling just before you stall as this is the time to pull airs and spins. Another variation when you get air is grabs. The part of the leg or skate you grab really is up to you – stalefish and hand plants are hot grabbing moves.

Whether you decide to play in an affiliated league or just street (pick-up) hockey with your mates you are in for a real blast.

Basic Gear

Do not rush out and buy all the gear. Whatever skates you have will be fine, and your armour from vert/street skating (a helmet is a must) will also suffice for a while. The only real bit of kit you may need is a stick (a regular hockey stick can even be used for a while), and a ball/puck. Only if you get really into the sport do you need to purchase specialist skates and pads.

Basic Rules

Players should wear protective gear at all times.

A team's maximum number of players allowed on the pitch at one time is five: one goalie and four outfielders (two defenders and two forwards).

Substitutions can be made all the time so even in large teams everyone can get some action. It also means that you can put all your energies into your short spell on the pitch.

The time limit for an international game is an hour, while an average game is 44 minutes with two twenty-minute halves and a four-minute break. 'Drop-in' games with friends have no time limits and can go on for hours.

A goal is scored when the ball passes completely over the line, between the two goal posts, but it doesn't count if it's kicked or thrown.

Before you start playing hockey, you need to learn the basic skills and shots.

Hockey Skills

The basic skills needed to play hockey are: skating backwards as well as you do forwards, stopping, turning and changing direction at will (all while keeping your head up). Additionally, you will need to be able to hold a stick and control a puck/ball.

The first skills you will need to learn are to control, dribble, pass and receive. Your stance is all important too. Getting it right will help you to balance — crucial in hockey.

Dribbling

Control and Dribble

Practise pushing the ball from side to side, cupping the ball so it doesn't bounce out of control. When confident, try skating slowly forward, transferring weight from leg to leg and moving the ball from side to side. Try not to look at what you are doing but feel the ball on your stick.

Passing

Being able to pass quickly and accurately is very important. Practise with a friend, skating around side by side and passing the ball to each other. Practise your hand—eye co-ordination, by bouncing the ball on the blade of the stick and seeing how many you can do.

Passing

Shooting

As with many sports, it's balls in the back of the net that count, so there are a few types of shot you need to master.

Wrist Shot

This is a quick shot, where you twist your body and put your weight onto your stick and skate nearest the ball. Quickly bring your arms forward and snap your wrists forward, propelling the ball towards the goal.

Sweep shot

that your weight is on your front foot and bring the ball forward with the blade. As the ball reaches the front of your body, hold the stick more firmly,

Slap Shot

This classic is a fast and powerful long-distance shot and a real crowd pleaser. The key to getting power is a big backswing.

Wrist shot

Forehand Sweep Shot

Spread your hands wide on the stick and bring the ball to your side, behind the back skate. Lean forward so

extend your arms and rotate your body. Tilt the blade up for a high shot and slightly cover the puck/ball for a low one.

Slap shot

Keeping your skates clean and doing a few checks once in a while is good practice. The good thing about skating is that, compared to other sports, maintenance costs are relatively low.

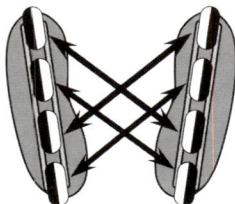

You will need:
- a toothbrush
- a tin for bearings
- a newspaper
- cleaning fluid (spirit-based)
- bearing oil
- a three-way spanner

Maintenance Routine

Keep all the bits you take off in order, clean them methodically and re-assemble them carefully. When everything is off the chassis, check the boot for cracks, wear and tear. Also look at buckles and laces and change them if they are looking worn or split. You do not want your boots coming off whilst pulling a huge air, nor to see your skate fly off into the distance just before you get served big style.

Wheel Rotation

It may seem like a complete hassle to undo all those wheel bolts (1) and rotate the order of those wheels, but a rotated wheel will last nearly four times as long as one that isn't. Take a look at the illustration

below on how to rotate your wheels between the skates. Whilst your wheels are out, take time to clean them (2). Pop out the bearings (3) and, if need be, clean them. Use a toothbrush to get dust and dirt off and, depending on type, strip them down. Bearings can be non-serviceable (NS) or fully serviceable (FS). For NS bearings, a toothbrushing and wipe down is all that's required.

Clean Bearings

A little more time and care is needed with FS bearings. First clean off

the outer grime, then pop the 'C' retaining clip and take off the protective shield, exposing the bearing. Toothbrush out crud and soak in a cleaner (4). Leave them to dry, then add a few drops of lubricant (5), replace the shield snap in the 'C' clip, add a bit of lubricant on the outside and reassemble the bearings in the wheel.

⚠️ **Skate Sense**

- Do not skate in the wet as water will get into your bearings, rust will result and your wheels will lock.

- Try not to skate through mud, gravel and sand as these will also get in and wreck the bearings.

- Use serviceable bearings as they last longer, saving you money.

- Be vigilant about tightening the bolts in your wheels, but do not over-tighten as you may squash the bearing case.

- If all-day sessions are your style carry a few spare parts and 3-way to replace or mini service your skate during the day.

- If you damage your inner boot don't worry as you can usually buy replacements.

- When you put your skates on, do up buckles and/or tuck in laces to avoid tripping on them.

- Service your bearings frequently, as it's these that keep you running smooth and true.

Acid drop A large fall or gap that you typically jump into or over – imagine dropping in on a vert.

Acid grind A grind in which your favoured foot is on the rail, but instead of your front foot being perpendicular to the bar, it points in the opposite direction.

Airtime When you're off the ground.

Alley oop Turning one way and spinning another, usually whilst catching air on a ramp.

Approach How you skate into a trick.

Armour Protective pads and guards.

Backside grind Grinding anything with your back facing the rail.

Bacon in the pan Crashing and sliding down a ramp and shrivelling up like frying bacon.

Blader A skater who does not do tricks.

Brainless A backflip with a 540° done on a ramp.

Bunny Novice skater who is always holding onto things.

Butter Smooth and flowing.

Carving Skating in a smooth arc.

Chassis Base of skate, where the wheels, brake and grind plate are found.

Cooked Skated to annihilation.

Coping Metal railings on top of a vert ramp, etc.

Crossovers Where feet cross over in a turn.

Disaster Usually, jumping high before landing and grinding.

Dropping in Entering ramp from the top.

Exit How you come out of a trick.

Fakie Doing anything (approach, exit, trick or spin) backwards.

Frame See chassis.

Frontside Jumping or moving onto an object/rail with legs apart.

Gherkin Beginner.

Glide A momentum-gaining way of skating.

Grind Sliding over surfaces on the chassis of the skate.

Grind plates Metal or composite plastic plates that fit into the chassis of aggressive skates.

Grom/Grommet Novice skater.

Halfpipe U-shaped ramp.

Hardcore Unafraid to take risks.

Jack To hit yourself on something whilst skating.

Glossary

Slalom Weaving movement (can be between cones).
Slamming Falling over whilst skating.
Soul grind A grind where the front foot is perpendicular like a normal frontside, but the back foot is parallel to the rail.
Spore Novice skater.
Stale Term used for any grab on the wheels.
Stalefish Reaching behind you to grab the outside of the opposite foot.
Street iron Stair rails etc. found for grinding whilst skating in public places.
Stroke A momentum-gaining way of skating.
Transition Part of ramp that takes you from vertical to horizontal.
Trouter Someone who brags.
Vanilla Plain, no frills.
Vert U-shaped ramp.
Zero spin Fakie with no spin.

Lid Helmet.
Mute Grabbing your boot on a jump.
Pads Protection (see armour).
Parallel 540⁰ High jump off the vert with a 540^0 spin.
Perp Streetlurker, pedestrian.
Planter Grabbing your boot in a jump.
Pros Professional skaters.
Pail Hand rail on stairs used for grinding.
Rambo laces Laces tied way too tight.

Rewind Spinning off a rail the opposite way you spun on.
Road rash Cuts and grazes from falling over.
Royale Like the frontside grind, but with your balance shifted backwards.
Scrape Stupid person on rental equipment.
Session Time spent skating on ramps, etc.
Sketchy A trick that was not landed well.
Skerd Skate nerd.
Skid-lid See lid.

Below are a few ideas to keep you fresh and up to date on the latest in tricks, skating stars and breaking news.

Magazines

Check out your local newsagent, or your local skate shop, which may have imported or hard-to-get mags from around the world. They carry a wealth of information and have breakdowns of new moves and skater profiles.

Internet

This is an obvious choice, just enter in-line skating in the search engine (e.g. www.google.com) and you're away. You could be even more specific and ask for tricks. The good thing about surfing is that you will hit companies who are totally up on the sport, and you can even e-mail them for advice.

Listed below are a few websites you might want to check out.

www.iisa.org This is the website for the International In-line Skating Association and is full of useful information.

www.aggroskate.com The website for fans of aggressive skating.

www.rollersports.org This website covers in-line skating events around the world.

www.skating.com An on-line magazine with loads of articles and information on skating.